W9-BRB-060

 Published in the United States by Golden Books, an imprint of Random House Children's Books, a division of Penguin Random House LLC, 1745 Broadway, New York, NY 10019, and in Canada by Random House of Canada, a division of Penguin Random House Ltd., Toronto. Golden Books, A Golden Book, A Little Golden Book, the G colophon, and the distinctive gold spine are registered trademarks of Penguin Random House LLC.

The artwork contained in this work was previously published in separate works by Golden Books, New York.

Cover illustration by Chris Kennett

randomhousekids.com

ISBN 978-0-7364-3656-4 (trade) — ISBN 978-0-7364-3657-1 (ebook)

MANUFACTURED IN CHINA
10 9 8 7 6 5 4 3

Everything I Need to Know I Learned From a STAR WARS® Little Golden Book

By Geof Smith

Illustrated by Alan Batson, Ethen Beavers, Ron Cohee, Chris Kennett, Heather Martinez, Caleb Meurer, Micky Rose, and Patrick Spaziante

A GOLDEN BOOK • NEW YORK

Does it feel like the weight of the galaxy is on your shoulders?

From *Star Wars: Return of the Jedi,* adapted by Geof Smith,
illustrated by Ron Cohee, © and ™ 2015 LUCASFILM LTD.

Are you being pulled in a direction that you don't want to go?

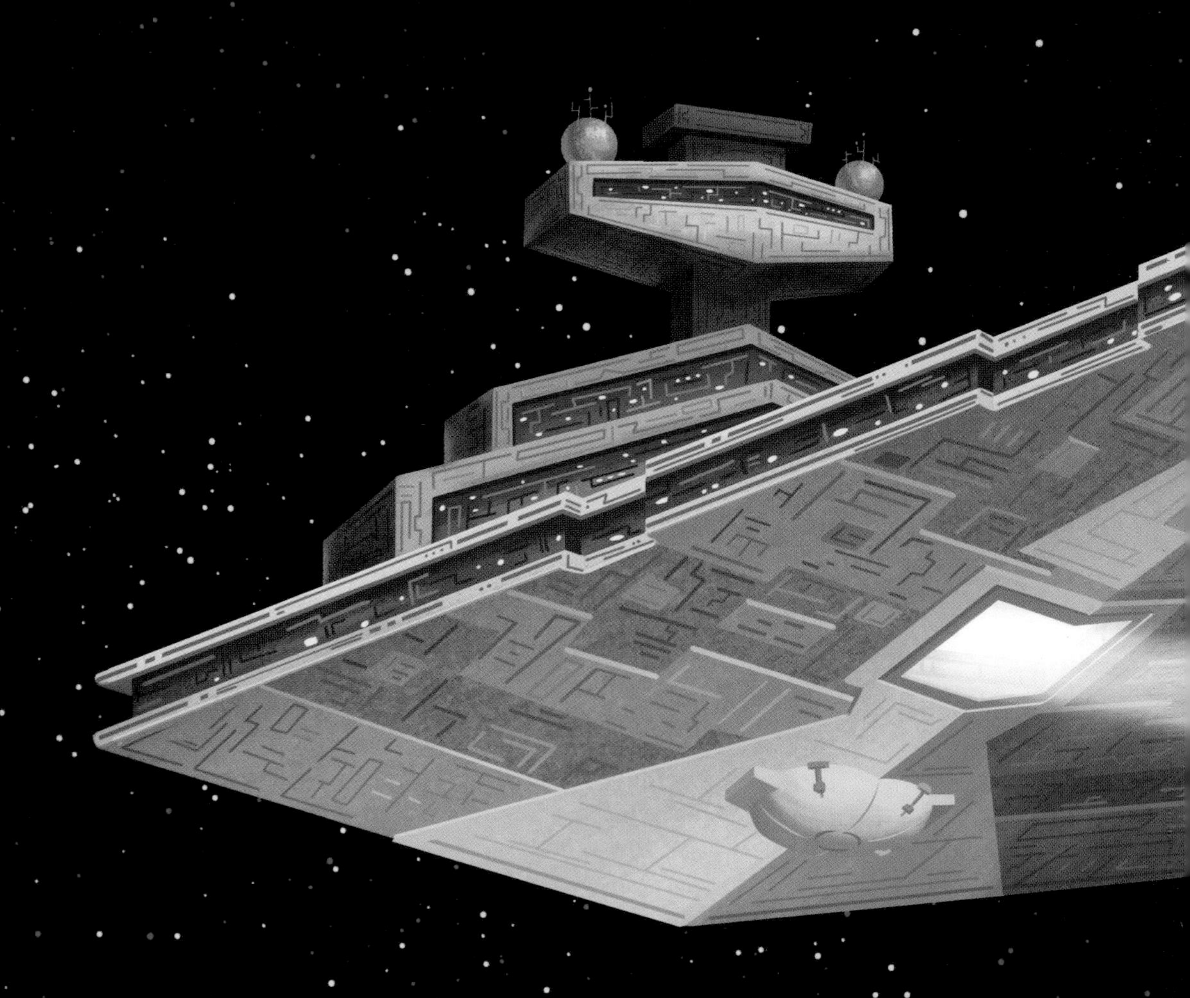

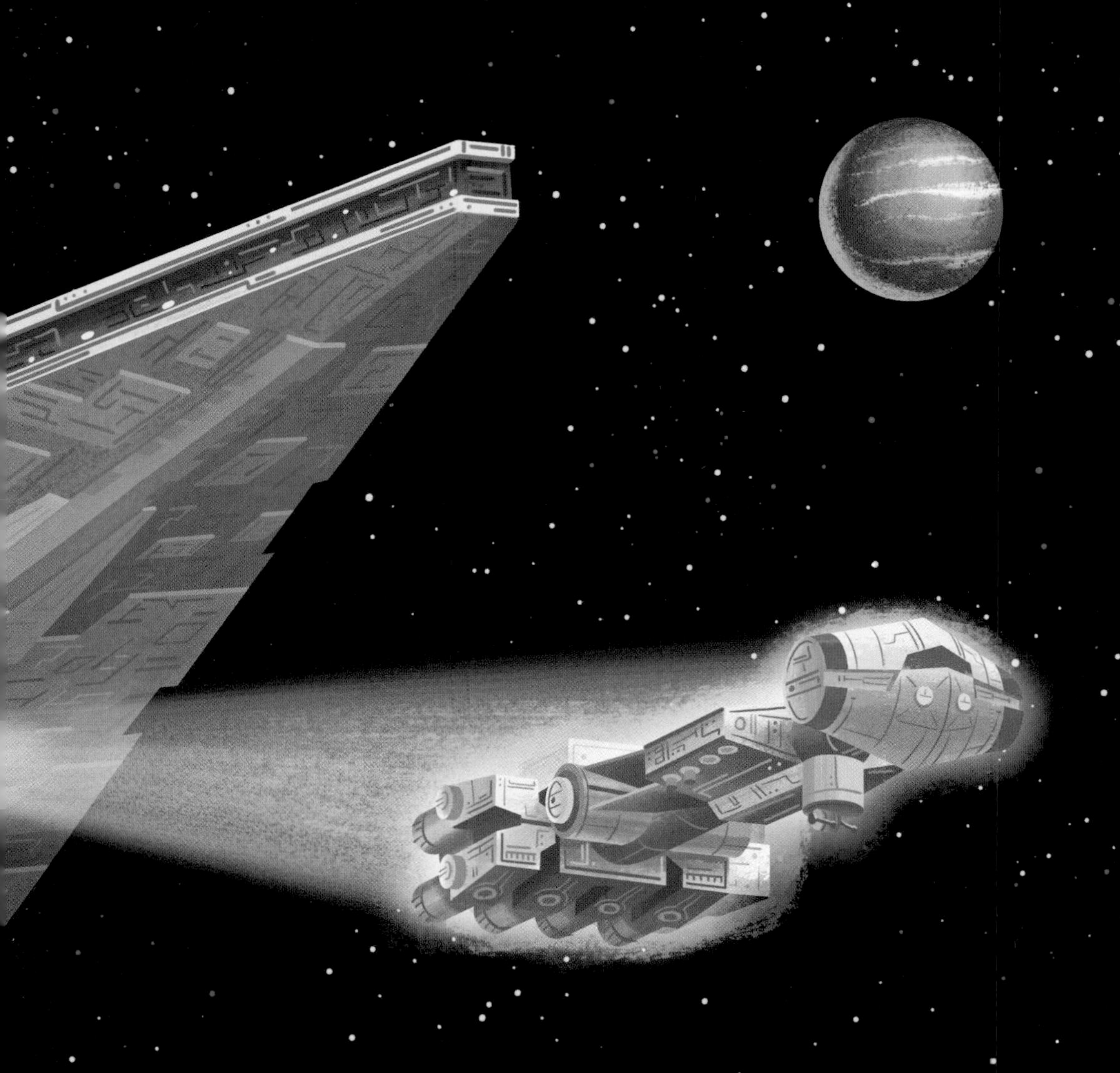

From *Star Wars: A New Hope,* adapted by Geof Smith,
illustrated by Caleb Meurer and Micky Rose,

Does it seem as if the walls are closing in . . .

and nobody understands you?

From *Star Wars: I Am a Droid,* by Christopher Nicholas,
illustrated by Chris Kennett,

(Even though you speak more than six million different languages.)

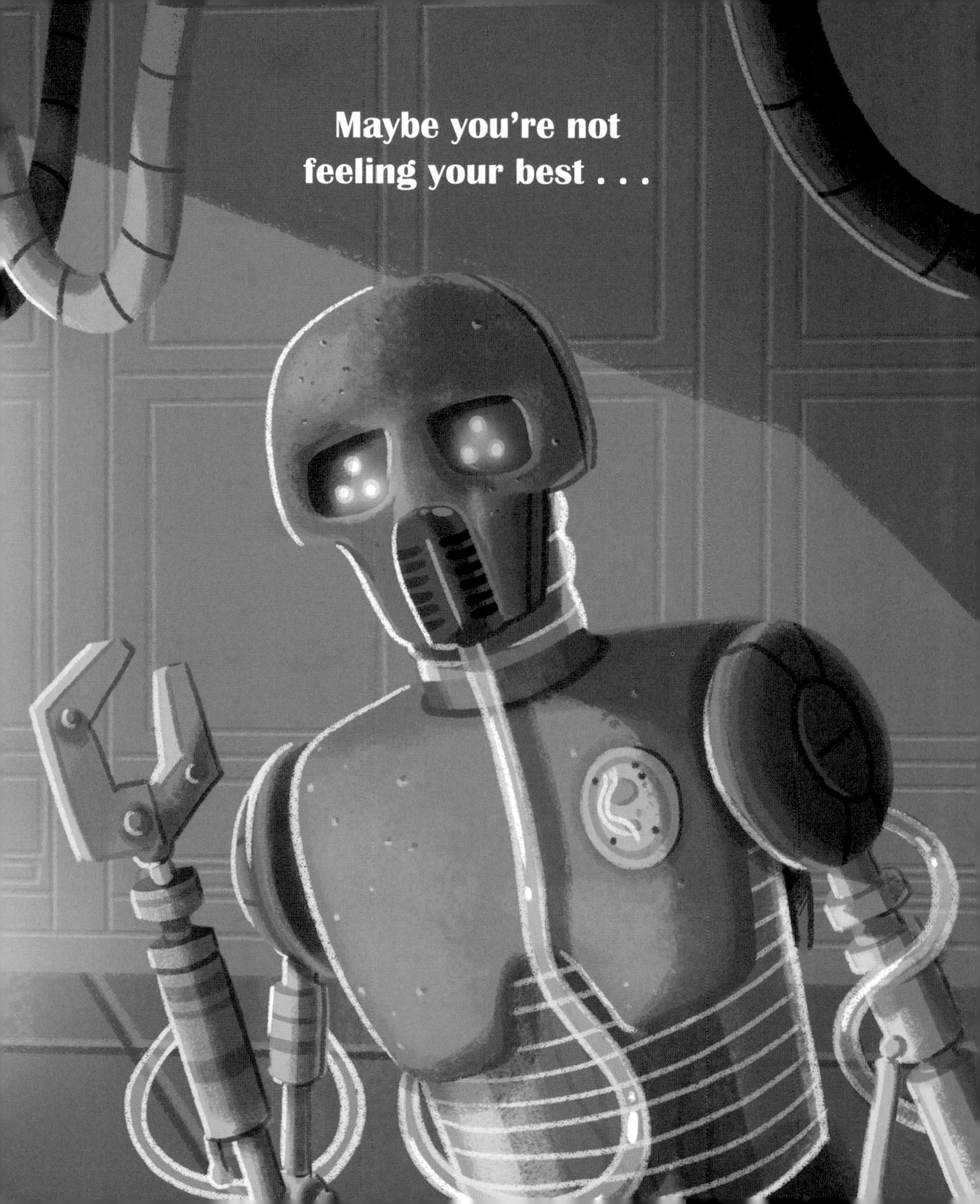
Maybe you're not
feeling your best . . .

like you're staring down the throat of the Sarlacc . . .

From *Star Wars: Return of the Jedi,* adapted by Geof Smith, illustrated by Ron Cohee, © and ™ 2015 LUCASFILM LTD.

and the odds of survival are 3,720 to one.

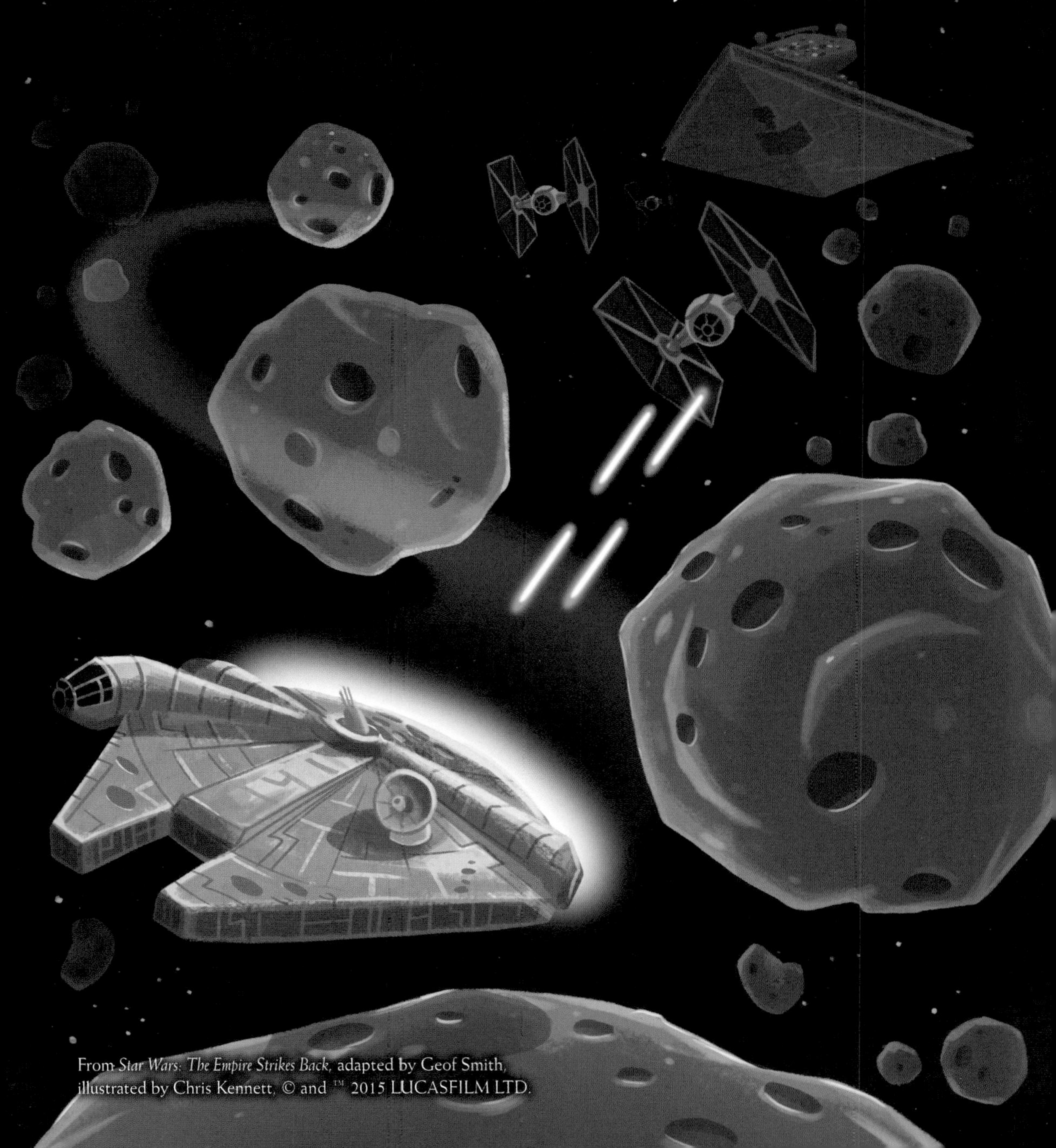

Because no matter where you are, on a desert planet . . .

or a frosty world of ice . . .

there will always be dark times.

Foes may appear when you least expect them.

From *Star Wars: Revenge of the Sith,* adapted by Geof Smith,
illustrated by Patrick Spaziante. © and ™ 2015 LUCASFILM LTD.

Dangers might block your way . . .

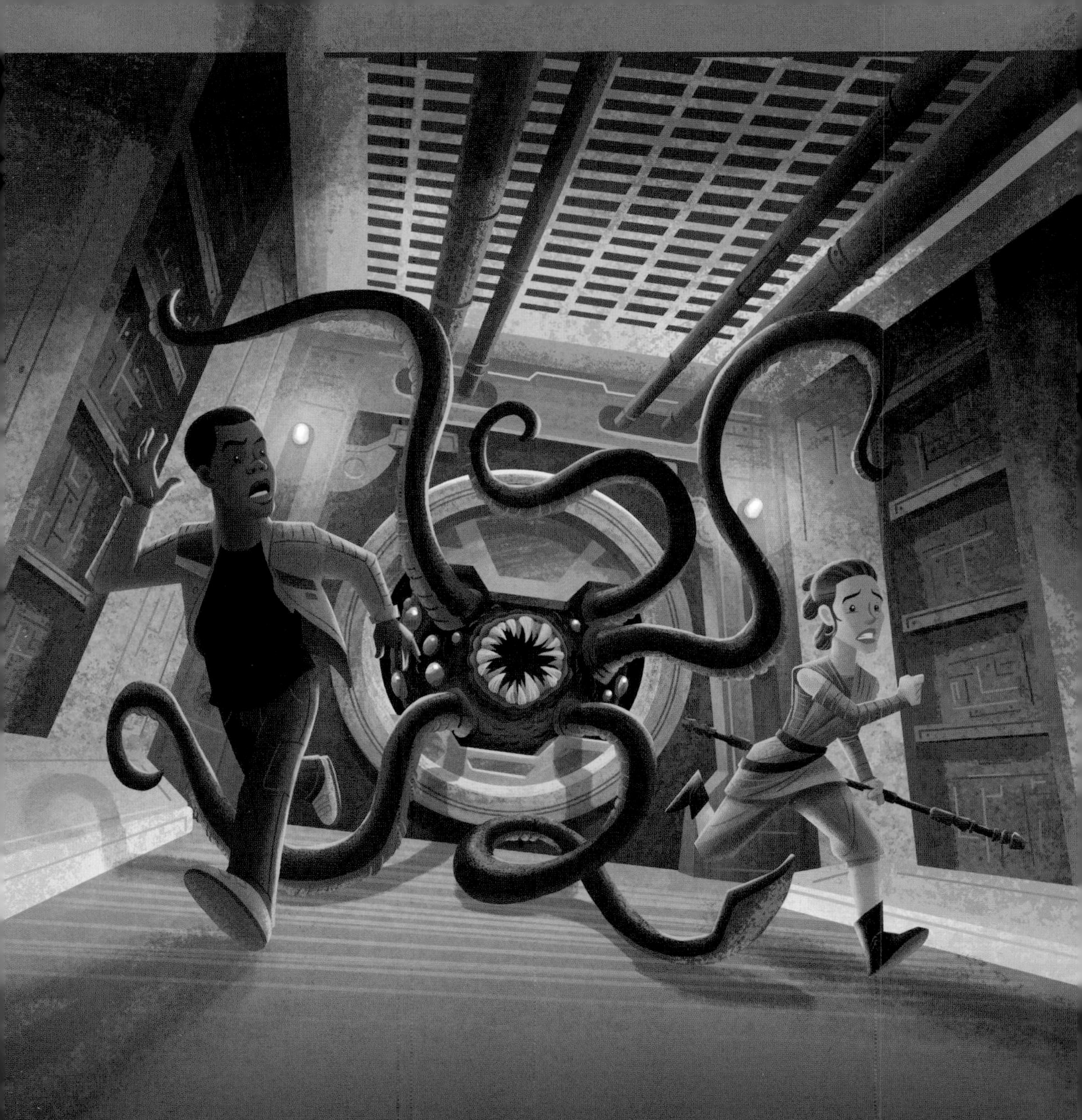

and there will be monstrous challenges.

From *Star Wars: Attack of the Clones,*
adapted by Christopher Nicholas,
illustrated by Ethen Beavers,

From *Star Wars: The Empire Strikes Back,* adapted by Geof Smith, illustrated by Chris Kennett,

From *Star Wars: I Am a Princess*,
by Courtney Carbone,
illustrated by Heather Martinez,

or *It's a trap!*

When life seems cold and lonely . . .

From *Star Wars: Attack of the Clones*,
adapted by Christopher Nicholas,
illustrated by Ethen Beavers,

Don’t back down.

And never give up your dreams.

If you believe that anything is possible . . .

there are distant worlds and amazing adventures awaiting you!

You may encounter noble knights . . .

From *Star Wars: I Am a Jedi,* by Christopher Nicholas,
illustrated by Ron Cohee, © and ™ 2016 LUCASFILM LTD.

or swashbuckling scoundrels.

And you can be a hero.

From *Star Wars: The Force Awakens,* adapted by Christopher Nicholas,
illustrated by Caleb Meurer and Micky Rose,

You might stand alone . . .

or with allies at your side.

You might be rescued
by someone special . . .

From *Star Wars: A New Hope,* adapted by Geof Smith, illustrated by Caleb Meurer and Micky Rose, © and ™ 2015 LUCASFILM LTD.

or rescue yourself!

But no matter how huge and overwhelming the galaxy may seem, always remember— size matters not.

Little droids can do big things.

A small child can save the day.

From *Star Wars: The Phanton Menace,* adapted by Courtney Carbone, illustrated by Heather Martinez, © and ™ 2015 LUCASFILM LTD.

Little friends can help you win great victories.

From *Star Wars: Return of the Jedi,* adapted by Geof Smith, illustrated by Ron Cohee, © and ™ 2015 LUCASFILM LTD.

Even tiny babies can hold a galaxy of hope.

Always believe in yourself and look inward.

Stay on target.

Because no matter how impossible a problem seems . . .

it will have a solution, if you look closely.

In fact, the biggest obstacles . . .

often have the simplest answers.

From *Star Wars: The Empire Strikes Back*,
adapted by Geof Smith, illustrated by Chris Kennett,

Success will eventually be yours!

You will get your just rewards.

But don't get cocky, kid.

Because one moment you're riding high on a tauntaun . . .

and the next moment you could be wampa food.

And on those days when nothing is going right . . .

From *Star Wars: I Am a Jedi,* by Christopher Nicholas, illustrated by Ron Cohee, © and ™ 2016 LUCASFILM LTD.

Don't get frustrated. Stay balanced and let the Force flow through you.

From *Star Wars: I Am a Jedi*,
by Christopher Nicholas,
illustrated by Ron Cohee,

can lead to
the dark side.

From *Star Wars: I Am a Sith,* by Christopher Nicholas,
illustrated by Chris Kennett,

The dark side may seem . . . impressive.

But what you will gain will not compare to what will be taken from you.

Once you kneel before the dark side . . .

it only leads to destruction . . .

From *Star Wars: The Force Awakens,*
adapted by Christopher Nicholas,
illustrated by Caleb Meurer
and Micky Rose,

From *Star Wars: The Empire Strikes Back,* adapted by Geof Smith, illustrated by Chris Kennett, © and ™ 2015 LUCASFILM LTD.

and hopelessness.

But even in the midst of darkness . . .

goodness can be found.

And no one is beyond saving.

Friends are never far away.

From *Star Wars: The Empire Strikes Back,* adapted by Geof Smith, illustrated by Chris Kennett,

From *Star Wars: The Empire Strikes Back,* adapted by Geof Smith,
illustrated by Chris Kennett.

inspire you with a good story . . .

or show you the way.

Because every trip is better with a good copilot . . .

and every challenge easier with a buddy by your side.

Create an alliance with someone special . . .

From *Star Wars: Attack of the Clones,* adapted by Christopher Nicholas, illustrated by Ethen Beavers,

and make the jump to lightspeed.

Friends and family will stand by you.

From *Star Wars: The Empire Strikes Back,* adapted by Geof Smith, illustrated by Chris Kennett,

And the Force will be with you, always.